Dear Parents:

Congratulations! Your child is taking the first steps on an exciting journey. The destination? Independent reading!

STEP INTO READING® will help your child get there. The program offers five steps to reading success. Each step includes fun stories and colorful art or photographs. In addition to original fiction and books with favorite characters, there are Step into Reading Non-Fiction Readers, Phonics Readers and Boxed Sets, Sticker Readers, and Comic Readers—a complete literacy program with something to interest every child.

Learning to Read, Step by Step!

Ready to Read   Preschool–Kindergarten
• big type and easy words • rhyme and rhythm • picture clues
For children who know the alphabet and are eager to begin reading.

Reading with Help   Preschool–Grade 1
• basic vocabulary • short sentences • simple stories
For children who recognize familiar words and sound out new words with help.

Reading on Your Own   Grades 1–3
• engaging characters • easy-to-follow plots • popular topics
For children who are ready to read on their own.

Reading Paragraphs   Grades 2–3
• challenging vocabulary • short paragraphs • exciting stories
For newly independent readers who read simple sentences with confidence.

Ready for Chapters   Grades 2–4
• chapters • longer paragraphs • full-color art
For children who want to take the plunge into chapter books but still like colorful pictures.

STEP INTO READING® is designed to give every child a successful reading experience. The grade levels are only guides; children will progress through the steps at their own speed, developing confidence in their reading. The F&P Text Level on the back cover serves as another tool to help you choose the right book for your child.

Remember, a lifetime love of reading starts with a single step!

All rights reserved. Published in the United States by Random House Children's Books, a division of Penguin Random House LLC, New York. Originally published in hardcover in the United States by Penguin Young Readers, an imprint of Penguin Random House LLC, New York, in 2018.

Based on the Llama Llama series by Anna Dewdney

Step into Reading, Random House, and the Random House colophon are registered trademarks of Penguin Random House LLC.

Visit us on the Web!
StepIntoReading.com
rhcbooks.com

Educators and librarians, for a variety of teaching tools, visit us at
RHTeachersLibrarians.com

Library of Congress Cataloging-in-Publication Data is available upon request.
ISBN 978-0-593-43260-0 (trade) — ISBN 978-0-593-43261-7 (lib. bdg.)

Printed in the United States of America
10 9 8 7 6 5 4 3 2 1

This book has been officially leveled by using the F&P Text Level Gradient™ Leveling System.

llama llama
Anna Dewdney
be my valentine!

based on the bestselling children's book series
by Anna Dewdney

Random House 🏠 New York

Llama Llama
is at school.
He is happy.
Tomorrow is
Valentine's Day!
He jumps for joy.

4

Zelda Zebra

is Llama Llama's teacher.

"Valentine's Day is a day to share

how much you care,"

says Zelda Zebra.

"To celebrate, we are going to have a party!"

says Zelda Zebra.

Each person in Llama's class

will make a special gift

to bring to the party.

It is time to have fun and

be creative!

Zelda Zebra tells everyone

to make something that

only *they* can make.

Luna Giraffe is busy

with her crafts.

She uses glitter,

ribbon, and colored

paper.

Gilroy Goat looks sadly at

his friend Luna.

"I have no idea what gift

to make," he says.

"I'm not very good with glitter."

Gilroy is worried.

What will he make for

his friends?

Llama Llama can help.
"There are so many
other things to make,"
says Llama.

How about a
sculpture from clay?

Oh no!

"I made a blob," says Gilroy.

"Maybe I should try something

besides art," he says.

Llama Llama goes home
after school.
He wants to make his Valentine's
gifts with Mama Llama.

Llama Llama invites Gilroy

to his house to help.

Maybe that will give Gilroy a new

idea of something he can make.

Llama says that he has an idea.

Llama wants to make yummy

cookies for his friends.

"I can make them

heart-shaped!"

he says.

"I'm ready to help,"

says Mama Llama.

"Me too!" shouts Gilroy.

Uh-oh!

Making cookies isn't so easy.

"Our cookies look like blobs!"

says Llama Llama.

Mama Llama has an idea.

"I say we make another batch,"

she says.

Next time they

will look like

hearts.

Llama Llama and Gilroy take a
break from baking to visit Luna.
She is making animals out of
paper for her gifts.
"I knew you would make
something fantastic!"
says Llama Llama.
"You are always so creative!"

The boys try to make

a paper bird.

Oh no!

Gilroy's bird doesn't look like

a bird at all!

"I better keep trying to find

something else I'm good at,"

says Gilroy.

At home, Llama Llama and

Gilroy make another batch

of cookies.

Oh no!

These cookies do not look like

hearts, either!

"This cookie looks like an octopus!" Llama says as he looks at his cookies.

"Don't worry.

We will try again," says Mama.

"While these cookies are baking, let's go visit Nelly to see what she is making,"

says Llama.

Llama and Gilroy go to

Nelly's house.

"It smells so good in here!"

says Gilroy.

"We're using cookie cutters to

make chocolate shapes,"

says Nelly.

Nelly came up

with a great gift!

Gilroy tries to make

a chocolate shape.

Gilroy makes a mess instead.

"Don't worry, Gilroy.

I know you'll find the right thing

to make," says Nelly.

On the way home, Llama Llama and Gilroy visit Euclid.

Euclid is making little buildings out of wooden sticks.

Wow!

"These buildings are so amazing!" says Llama Llama.

24

But Gilroy can't build anything

like that for his friends.

He is not great at math

like Euclid is.

"You have to figure out your *own*

thing," says Llama Llama.

"I know that you will come up

with something great!"

says Euclid.

The Valentine's Day party is finally here!

"What amazing and original valentines!" says Zelda Zebra.

"I made heart-shaped cookies for everyone," says Llama Llama. "You just have to use your imagination on the heart part!" he says.

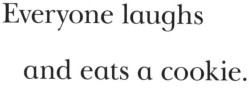

Everyone laughs and eats a cookie.

There is one more gift to give out.

It is a Valentine's Day card.

But these aren't just *any*

Valentine's Day cards.

There are

poems inside!

Llama Llama reads his card
out loud.

It says he is a great friend.

"I love my poem!" he says.

"Did you get a poem, Gilroy?"

asks Luna.

Gilroy shrugs.

Wait!

Llama Llama understands.

"It was *you*!

You wrote the poems!"

Llama Llama shouts.

"This is what you made for

Valentine's Day," he says.

Gilroy smiles proudly.

"You told me to do something

that was creative and *me*!

And I love writing!" he says

to Zelda Zebra.

"And you are so good at it!

I hope you do a lot more

of it," says Zelda Zebra.

What a special Valentine's Day.

Llama Llama and his classmates

show one another

how much they care—

and they discover their own

special talents!